For my gorgeous Lucy and Amy x

All rights reserved. Published by Scholastic Press, an imprint of Scholastic Inc.,
Publishers since 1920. SCHOLASTIC, SCHOLASTIC PRESS, and associated logos
are trademarks and/or registered trademarks of Scholastic Inc.

The publisher does not have any control over and does not assume any
responsibility for author or third-party websites or their content.

The Three Little Superpigs was originally published in Great Britain by
Fourth Wall Publishing in 2016 under the title *The Three Little Superpigs*.

This book is a work of fiction. Names, characters, places, and incidents are either the
product of the author's imagination or are used fictitiously, and any resemblance to actual persons,
living or dead, business establishments, events, or locales is entirely coincidental.

Library of Congress Cataloging-in-Publication Data available

ISBN 978-1-338-24545-5

10 9 8 7 6 5 4 3 2 1   18 19 20 21 22

Printed in China   38

This edition first printing, August 2018

The Three Little SUPERPIGS

Written and illustrated by
Claire Evans

Scholastic Press • New York

Once upon a time, there were three little pigs who captured the Big Bad Wolf in the house made of bricks. The hungry Wolf fell down the little pigs' chimney into a big pan of boiling water! He huffed and he puffed . . . but it was no use!

He had fallen right into the pigs' trap!

"I'll get you one day, little pigs!"
the angry Wolf shouted as he was
carted off to prison.
With smiles on their snouts,
the three little pigs waved good-bye
to the big bad villain.

The citizens of Fairyland were very happy that the Big Bad Wolf had been defeated. The little pigs were awarded special "superhero" status and became known as "THE THREE LITTLE SUPERPIGS." Working together, they all rebuilt the whole town out of bricks to keep everyone safe.

"We love you, SUPERPIGS!"

From that moment on, the SUPERPIGS spent all their days
being heroes and enjoying their newfound fame.
When they weren't greeting their fans, they were fighting crime
and stopping nursery rhyme bad guys.

Meanwhile,
deep inside "Happily Never After Prison,"
the very angry Big Bad Wolf
was hungrily plotting his revenge
in his cold and dreary cell.

THE PIE POST

BIG BAD WOLF
CAUGHT
SUPERPIGS
SAVE FAIRYLAND

A few weeks later, the SUPERPIGS were called to investigate a new crime. Mysteriously, one by one, bricks were starting to disappear all around Fairyland. This was very strange!

The SUPERPIGS were on the case!

HOUSE #3

RAPUNZEL'S TOWER

SP2

MISSING BRICKS
RAPUNZEL'S TOWER
BRICK TOWN ROAD
RED DOOR HOUSE

Crime Scene Do Not Cross

Crime Scene Do Not Cross

Not Cross

Later that day, they received some shocking news . . .

"THE BIG BAD WOLF HAS ESCAPED!"

The residents of Fairyland were scared
and once again turned to the SUPERPIGS for help.
"Don't worry," the three heroes boasted,
"we'll find that Wolf and make him pay!"

The three little SUPERPIGS hunted high and low,
far and wide, and long and hard,
but the Big Bad Wolf was nowhere to be seen.

The pigs searched everywhere for clues!

Some people claimed they'd seen
the Wolf dressed up as an old lady . . .

. . . so the pigs rounded up all the grandmas in Fairyland.

But the Wolf was a master
of disguise and they just
couldn't spot him!

Every day, more and more bricks disappeared
from Fairyland. As night fell, the whole town
locked themselves indoors, too frightened to go out.
They hoped the SUPERPIGS would find the Wolf soon.
He was up to something big and bad!

Back at home, the first SUPERPIG was relaxing
when he sensed something strange.
Suddenly, a dark shadow fell upon the room . . .

"THE BIG BAD WOLF!"
cried the SUPERPIG.

"I don't need to huff, I don't need to puff, and I don't need to blow your house in . . .
Because I'm already inside!" replied the pointy-eared Wolf.
The pig ran out through the front door, but was met with a terrible surprise!

The cunning Wolf had built
a gigantic wall around the SUPERPIGS' houses
using the stolen bricks from Fairyland!
The SUPERPIG was trapped.

Attempting to flee,
the SUPERPIG tried to climb
the brick wall using a ladder
from the side of his house —
but it was too short!

"Gotcha!"

sneered the Wolf
as he captured the
helpless pig.

Unaware of the danger, the second SUPERPIG was at home polishing his medals, when he suddenly spotted something out of the corner of his eye . . .

"THE BIG BAD WOLF!"

shrieked the
SUPERPIG.

"I don't need to huff.
I don't need to puff. I don't need to
blow your house down . . .
Because I am already inside!"
growled the Wolf.

With a huge scream,
the terrified SUPERPIG
quickly ran outside and into
the enormous brick wall!

Desperate to escape, the little pig jumped on a nearby trampoline,
bouncing as high as he could . . . but it was no use!

"Gotcha!" boasted the Wolf as he caught the pig in his trusty net.

"Two down, one to go!"
laughed the Wolf as he
prepared his delicious meal.

The third SUPERPIG had heard all the commotion
and was busy hatching a plan when
the Big Bad Wolf suddenly appeared at his window!

The SUPERPIG grabbed his gear,
raced straight out the front door
and down the path as quickly as his
little legs could carry him.

Working quickly, he freed his captured brothers from their tight pastry blankets. But it was not quick enough!

"HA! HA! HA! There's nowhere to run
and nowhere to hide—I've built a wall around
your houses, and now you're trapped inside!"
laughed the hungry Wolf.

"You're no SUPERPIGS . . .
You're my dinner!"

"I DON'T THINK SO!"
shouted the third SUPERPIG!
He whispered to his brothers . . .
"Ready, set, let's go!"
And in a flash . . .

... they blasted off, high into the night sky!

The clever brother had outsmarted the silly Wolf again!
Using his jet pack invention to save the day,
the SUPERPIGS had left the Big Bad Wolf trapped
in his own self-built brick prison.

The angry Wolf
raised his fists ...

"I'll get you yet,
little pigs!"

Up in the sky, the three SUPERPIGS laughed out loud—
"You'll never get us. Not by the hairs on our chinny-chin-chins!"

And down below, the citizens of Fairyland cheered—

"Wow, pigs really can fly!"

The three little pigs had saved Fairyland from the
Big Bad Wolf once again. They truly were superheroes!
"Hooray for the Three Little
SUPERPIGS!"

The End?